For Dara

JANETTA OTTER-BARRY BOOKS

Dreams copyright © Frances Lincoln Limited 2013
Text and illustrations copyright © Shirin Adl 2013

First published in Great Britain in 2013 and in the USA in 2014 by
Frances Lincoln Children's Books, 4 Torriano Mews,
Torriano Avenue, London NW5 2RZ
www.franceslincoln.com

A catalogue record for this book is available from the British Library.

ISBN 978-1-84780-383-2

Illustrated with watercolour, collage, coloured pencil

Printed in Dongguan, Guangdong, China by Toppan Leefung in January, 2013

9 8 7 6 5 4 3 2 1

The Book of DrEAms

Shirin Adl

F

FRANCES LINCOLN
CHILDREN'S BOOKS

Dreams come in many different shapes and forms...

Some dreams are nice and simple.

Fork and Spoon

Go back home

Umbrellas for sale

Some dreams are

scary!

But even those ones can be fun!

In our dreams sometimes we can do things

that we are not normally

able to do,

like breathing underwater

or flying in the sky.

In a dream anything is possible.

We can pick clouds
from the top of a mountain...

travel back in time.

or talk to animals.

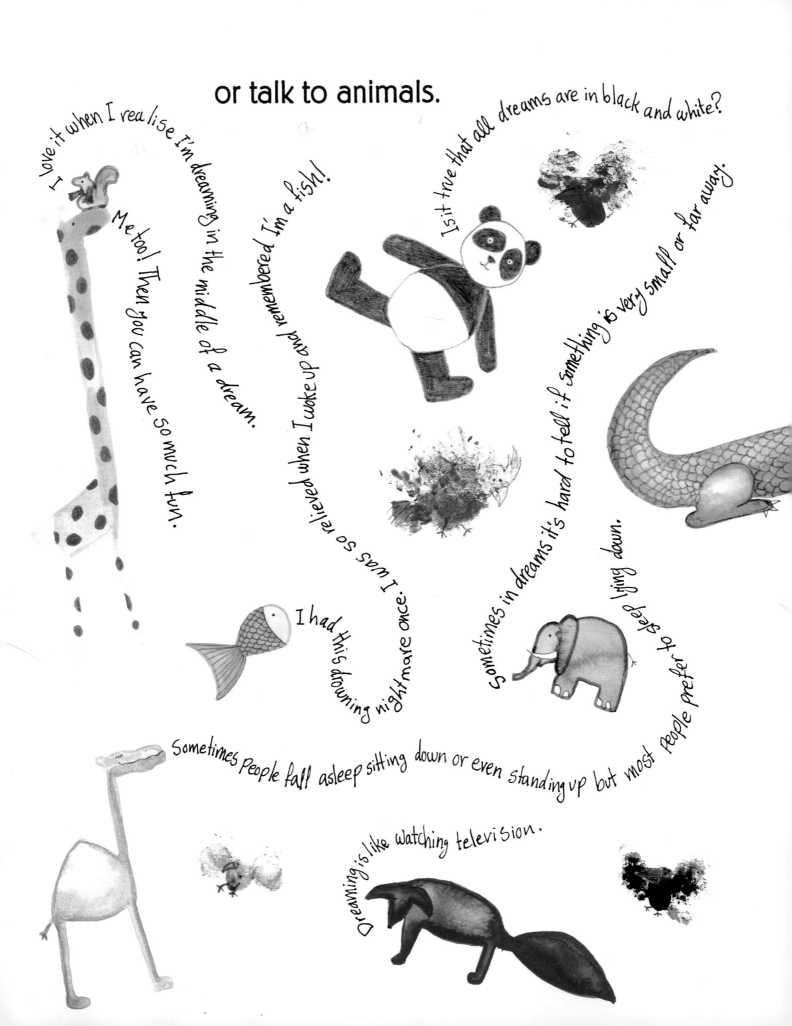

I love it when I realise I'm dreaming in the middle of a dream.

Me too! Then you can have so much fun.

I was so relieved when I woke up and remembered I'm a fish!

Is it true that all dreams are in black and white?

Sometimes in dreams it's hard to tell if something is very small or far away.

I had this drowning nightmare once.

Sometimes in dreams it's hard to tell if something is very small or far away.

Most people prefer to sleep lying down.

Sometimes people fall asleep sitting down or even standing up but most people prefer to sleep lying down.

Dreaming is like watching television.

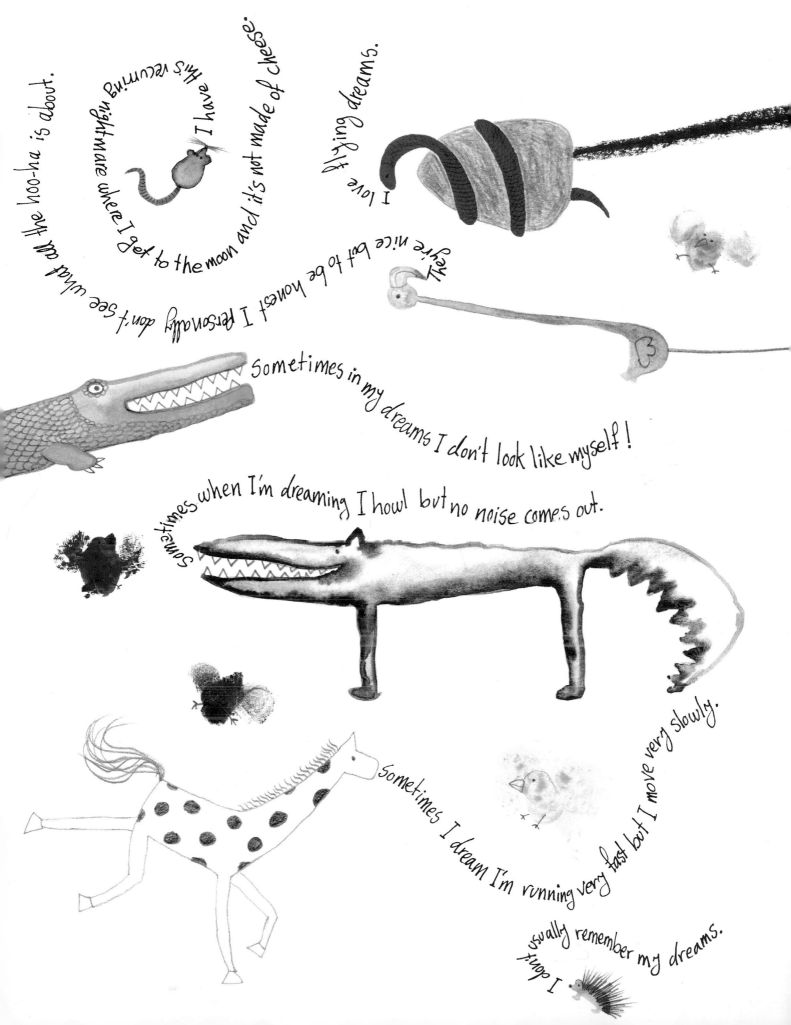

I have His recurring nightmare where I get to the moon and it's not made of cheese. I have fall what the hoo-ha is about.

I love flying dreams.

They're nice but to be honest I personally don't see what

Sometimes in my dreams I don't look like myself!

Sometimes when I'm dreaming I howl but no noise comes out.

Sometimes I dream I'm running very fast but I move very slowly.

I don't usually remember my dreams.

Maybe you've had a dream

Or where you are very small

and everything else is very **big.**

Dreams make our night-times
more exciting because they come
in many different shapes and forms.

Do you remember
what you
dreamed about
last night?

What do you think you'll dream about tonight?